Mega Military Machines™

SUBMARINES

Catherine Ellis

PowerKiDS
press™
New York

Published in 2007 by The Rosen Publishing Group, Inc.
29 East 21st Street, New York, NY 10010

First Edition

Editor: Amelie von Zumbusch
Book Design: Greg Tucker

Photo Credits: Cover © AFP/AFP/Getty Images; p. 5 © Phil Mislinski/Getty Images; p. 7 © Julian Herbert/Getty Images; p. 9 U.S. Navy file photo; p. 11 image copyright Daniel Gale, 2006. Used under license from Shutterstock, Inc.; p. 13 Department of Defense; p. 15 © Toru Yamanaka/AFP/Getty Images; p. 17 © China Photos/Getty Images; p. 19 by Mass Communication Specialist Seaman Joshua Martin, U.S. Navy; p. 21 by Journalist 1st Class Jason E. Miller, U.S. Navy; p. 23 by Petty Officer 2nd Class Steven H. Vanderwerff, U.S. Navy. Department of Defense.

Library of Congress Cataloging-in-Publication Data

Ellis, Catherine.
   Submarines / Catherine Ellis. — 1st ed.
      p. cm. — (Mega military machines)
   Includes index.
   ISBN-13: 978-1-4042-3665-3 (library binding)
   ISBN-10: 1-4042-3665-1 (library binding)
   1. Submarines (Ships)—Juvenile literature. I. Title.
   V857.E45 2007
   623.825'7—dc22

                                                    2006029635

Manufactured in the United States of America

Contents

Submarines are boats that can go underwater. They can dive down as deep as 1,600 feet (488 m).

5

The people who work on military submarines are part of the **navy**.

Submarines are very big. You can see their full size only when they are on dry land to be fixed or cleaned, though.

9

The navy uses submarines to watch ships from unfriendly countries secretly.

A submarine's shape lets it move easily through the water.

Submarines often move slowly so that they make little noise. However, they can go as fast as 29 miles per hour (47 km/h).

15

The navy uses submarines to fire **missiles**. Submarines can even fire missiles when they are underwater.

Submarines have a **periscope**. A periscope lets you see what is going on outside of the submarine.

Submarines have big **propellers**. A submarine's propellers spin to move the boat through the water.

Some submarines can come up through a big sheet of ice!

Words to Know

missiles (MIH-sulz) Things that are shot at something far away.

navy (NAY-vee) A group of sailors who are trained to fight at sea.

periscope (PER-ih-skohp) A tool that is used to see above the top of the water from underwater.

propellers (pruh-PEL-erz) Paddlelike parts on an object that spin to move the object forward.

Index

Web Sites

Due to the changing nature of Internet links, PowerKids Press has developed an online list of Web sites related to this book. This site is updated regularly. Please use this link to access the list:
www.powerkidslinks.com/mmm/sub/